Thanks to
Asako Schluckebier and Keiko Watanabe,
whose generous assistance made
this book possible

For Silke, Susan, Patti,
Pat, and Josie, whose unending love
and support are more precious than any pearl

D. P.

Copyright © 1997 by Daniel Powers

First edition 1997

Library of Congress Cataloging-in-Publication Data

Powers, Daniel.
Jiro's pearl / Daniel Powers. — 1st ed.
Summary: When he sets off to get medicine for his sick grandmother, a poor
country boy in long-ago Japan begins an adventure that teaches him
the value of duty, trust, and generosity.
ISBN 1-56402-631-0
[1. Fairy tales. 2. Japan—Fiction.] I. Title.
PZ8.P865Ji   1996
[E]—dc20   95-47615

2 4 6 8 10 9 7 5 3 1

Printed in Italy

This book was typeset in Calligraph 810.
The pictures were done in watercolor.

Candlewick Press
2067 Massachusetts Avenue
Cambridge, Massachusetts 02140

Daniel Powers

JIRO'S PEARL

CANDLEWICK PRESS
CAMBRIDGE, MASSACHUSETTS

A long time ago in a land across the sea lived a kindhearted boy named Jiro. His grandmother cared for him in an old farmhouse at the edge of a pond. They were poor country folk, but were very happy together.

One morning Jiro awoke to find his grandmother still in bed, sick with fever.

"Jiro," whispered the old woman, "go to the tea chest and open the second bin. There you will find the last of our fine white rice. Take the rice to the market to sell. With the money you receive, ask the yakuzaishi to prepare some medicine for me. But do not stop along the way."

Jiro found the fine white rice just as his grandmother had said. He poured it into a sack, bowed deeply to his grandmother, and set out for the village.

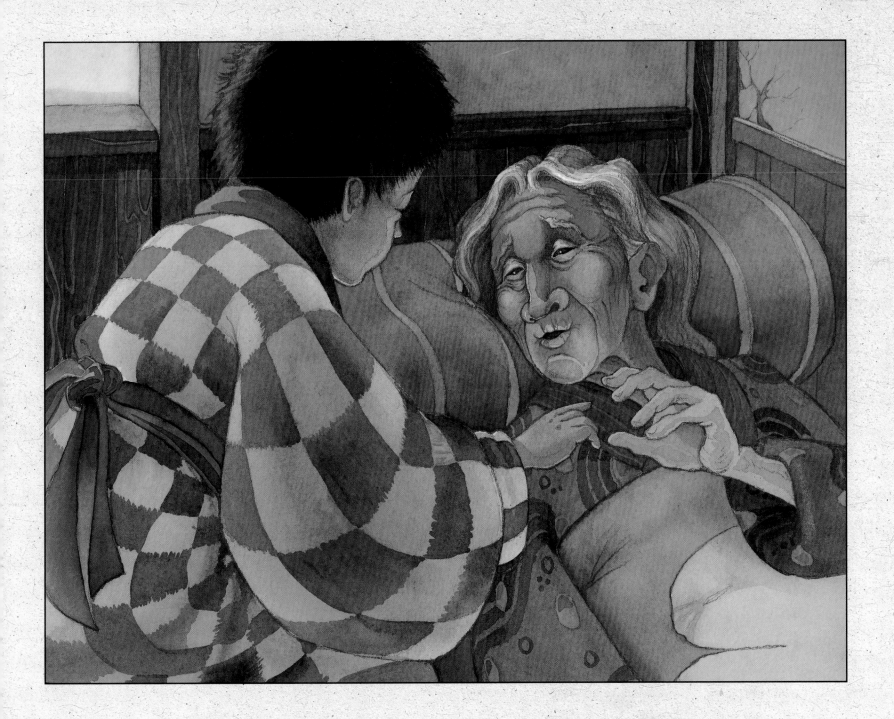

Along the way Jiro paid no attention to the path beneath his feet or to the squawking crows above his head. Thoughts of his task in the village filled his mind.

All at once a toad jumped onto the path. Jiro shouted with joy, for he loved no creature more than the toad. Dropping the rice, Jiro chased it, until finally he caught the warty thing and tucked it safely into the sleeve of his kimono. But when he returned to gather up the bag of rice, Jiro found several crows greedily gobbling down the last grains.

He knew that without rice he could not buy medicine for his grandmother.

With a sinking heart, he remembered his grandmother's parting words: "Do not stop along the way."

Frantic, Jiro raced to the yakuzaishi.

"Please, Yakuzaishi-san, Grandmother is very ill and needs medicine. But I disobeyed her — I lost the rice that I was to sell at the market, so now I have no money to buy medicine. Please, could you help me?"

The white-haired man stared at Jiro. "I can help you," he replied. "But you must do exactly as I tell you."

He was silent for a moment, then said, "Follow the street to the bay, where you will find a boat strewn with fishing nets. Untie it and row out from the shore. When you reach the middle of the bay, call into the water to a fish that swims there. Tell it your troubles and it will help you. In return for my advice, I ask that you not forget me as you forgot your grandmother's request."

Jiro vowed not to forget the yakuzaishi. Then he followed the street to the bay, where he found the boat. He untied it, rowed to the middle of the bay, and called:

"I've wandered astray,
*   Great Fish from the bay;*
I need your assistance,
*   Please do not delay!"*

Suddenly, a big beautiful fish sprang, splashing into the boat. Jiro shivered with excitement.

"Great Fish from the bay," he began. "Grandmother is ill and needs medicine, but because I disobeyed her I cannot buy any. Could you help me?"

The fish stared at Jiro, then said, "I can help you, but you must do exactly as I tell you." Then it said, "Follow me," and to Jiro's horror, the fish dove back into the sea!

Thinking of his sick grandmother, Jiro gathered his courage, took a deep breath, and jumped overboard after the fish.

Down, down they swam into the icy green water. Goosebumps covered Jiro's body and thousands of tiny bubbles tickled his skin. To his delight, he found that he could breathe underwater.

The fish darted ahead of Jiro, who kicked furiously to keep up.

The fish finally slowed and steered Jiro to an enormous oyster. Inside the oyster was a pearl larger than a paper lantern.

"Jiro-chan," said the fish, "this pearl shall be your fortune." With the help of the fish, Jiro pushed and pulled, then popped the pearl free, and the two returned with it to the boat.

"In exchange for my help," said the fish, "I have two things to ask of you: Do not forget me as you forgot your grandmother's request; and do not sell this pearl under any circumstance."

With a swish of its tail, the fish disappeared into the water.

"But how am I to buy Grandmother's medicine if I cannot sell this pearl?" cried Jiro. "What am I to do?"

Jiro returned to the village, burdened by his troubles and the large but useless pearl. As he rounded a corner, Jiro nearly stumbled over a beggar. At first Jiro was frightened, but he had often seen his grandmother feed and clothe beggars. With this in mind, he gave the man his pearl.

"This pearl cannot help my grandmother, but I think that it could help you. Please take it and with it make your fortune," Jiro said.

Smiling, the man bowed in humble thanks.

At that moment, the toad jumped out of Jiro's sleeve. It hopped once, twice, three times, and then it turned into the most beautiful woman Jiro had ever seen. The air became heavy with the scent of jasmine. Jiro's heart raced.

"Young Jiro-chan," the woman said, "at long last you have learned the importance of doing what is asked of you. And you have demonstrated your kindness by helping this beggar. Your faithfulness will restore your grand-mother's health and bring forth all the treasures you could want. Be proud of yourself, Jiro-chan." And with these words, the woman changed into a swallow and flew off over the rooftops.

When Jiro returned home, he was surprised to find his grandmother busy preparing for tea.

"Grandmother!" cried Jiro as he raced to hug her. "You are well."

"Yes, Jiro-chan. And I think it is due to a peculiar dream I just had. I dreamed a swallow flew through my window and placed a pink pearl in my mouth. When I awoke, I was well."

His grandmother's dream did not surprise Jiro, and he told her of his odd adventures. As he finished, the water for the tea began to boil. Grandmother took the pot from the fire and reached for the tea in the chest next to her.

When she opened the chest, the house echoed with tings, pings, and *tat-a-tat-tats* as jewels spilled onto the floor! Then out flowed fish, rice, and soba noodles. Green tea, sake, and plum wine. Kimonos, happi coats, and geta sandals. Pearls, jade, and ivory. Gold, silver, and cinnabar.

"Grandmother!" cried Jiro.

"Jiro!" cried Grandmother. "All the treasures the woman spoke of! We will never be needy again!"

To this day, the villagers still wonder how an old beggar's fortune was so mysteriously changed—so too, an old woman's and her grandson's. Some say they stole their riches, some say they inherited them, some say they received them as a gift. But only those as kind-hearted and faithful as Jiro will ever know the real story.